Jessica Moffat's
Silver Locket

For Katherine:

I hope you enjoy the book

Alan M——

Jun 15/95

To Katherine
with best wishes

Michael Martchenko.

Jessica Moffat's Silver Locket

by Allen Morgan
illustrated by Michael Martchenko

Stoddart

First published in 1994 by
Stoddart Publishing Co. Limited
34 Lesmill Road
Toronto, Canada
M3B 2T6
(416) 445-3333

Canadian Cataloguing in Publication Data

Morgan, Allen, 1946–
Jessica Moffat's silver locket

Hardcover ISBN 0-7737-2840-6
Paperback ISBN 0-7737-5701-5

I. Martchenko, Michael.   II. Title.

PS8576.064J4 1994   jC813'.54   C94-930295-3
PZ7.M67Je 1994

Printed in Hong Kong

When Jessica Moffat was seven, her grandmother died. A few weeks later Jessica's mother gave her the locket her grandmother always wore.

"It's been in the family for many years," she said. "Your grandmother's grandmother gave it to her. Now it's yours."

"Grandmum used to let me hold it sometimes," Jessica whispered. "She told me there would be something important I'd want to put in it some day."

The locket was dented and looked very old. When Jessica tried to pry it open with her fingernails, the clasp wouldn't budge. But even though it had seen better days, to Jessica it was very special. Whenever she was feeling worried, she held it tight in the palm of her hand and everything seemed to turn out all right.

Jessica was holding her locket very tight the night her father called the family meeting. The news wasn't good. His business was in trouble.

"We'll have to tighten our belts for a while and spend a lot less than we usually do until I can save enough money to buy the computers I need," he told them.

"Have we run out of money?" Jessica asked with a worried frown.

"It's not as bad as that," said her mother with a trace of a smile. "You're always such a worrier, Jess. We'll manage."

"I've been saving my allowance up. You can use that," Jessica offered. "We could have a garage sale too. I bet we'd make lots."

"Nothing we own would be worth what I need," her father explained.

"Oh, I wouldn't say that," said Jessica's granddad.

Everyone turned and looked in surprise. Jessica's granddad had been sitting so still, they had forgotten he was even there.

"There is one thing we could sell; a stamp I gave to your grandmother, Jess. I haven't thought of it for years, but I'm sure it's still up in the attic somewhere."

"A Stamp! Some stamps are valuable, aren't they mum?" Jessica asked.

"I suppose," said her mother, but it was easy to see that she really didn't think so. Neither did Jessica's dad.

"This one will bring in a bundle," Granddad said.
"It was worth a good price fifty years ago,
and you know how it is. The older things get,
the better they are — just like people."

Later that evening when Jessica was ready for bed, her granddad came to say goodnight. He found her looking at the silver locket. "I wish I could open it up and see what Grandmum kept inside," she said. "She told me once that this locket was like a door to her heart and she kept the key inside. But what good is a key if it's locked away? How could a locket be a door? It's much too small."

Granddad smiled. "An acorn is small, but it has a whole tree inside."

"I suppose," Jessica agreed, squeezing the locket tight. "Do you think the stamp you gave to Grandmum is worth enough money to help Dad out?"

"Absolutely. Why I still remember crystal clear the day I gave it to her. It was such a very long time ago, Jess."

"Before I was born?"

"Way before that, before your mother was born, in fact. I hadn't married your grandmother yet. I was going away to fight in the war and she came to see me off. I wanted to leave something special for her. My stamp collection was the most valuable thing I owned right then, so I gave her that. One of the stamps, the expensive one, reminded her of me. The man on the stamp had a moustache, you see, and I did too. What she really wanted was a photo I think, but I didn't have one."

"Grandmum was neat," Jessica said, feeling the locket grow warm in her hand. "I miss her sometimes."

"So do I," her granddad agreed.

When Jessica came home from school the next day she found her grandfather waiting for her with the stamp album.

"It's gone!" he moaned. "Look!"

Jessica looked. There, in the middle of the page, was an empty space where a stamp had once been. She knew right away which one was missing.

"Grandmum must have hidden it somewhere," Jessica said.

"How will I ever find it now? I should have known this would never work. Your parents knew. They think I'm getting too old to help. Maybe I am."

"No. You're not," Jessica told him, "but I know just how you feel. Mum and Dad think I'm too young. Don't worry, we'll find that stamp if we have to search the whole house."

Jessica helped her grandfather look, but when it was finally time for bed, the stamp was still missing.

As Jessica lay awake in the dark, she could hear her parents talking in the kitchen. She was certain something dreadful was going to happen. *If Dad isn't able to get enough money, we might have to sell our house,* she worried. *We might even have to move away to a whole different city. Where would we go?*

Jessica knew it wasn't that bad. She tried to imagine happier things, but the terrible feelings just grew and grew. Finally she closed her eyes and squeezed her silver locket tight.

"I wish I could be with Grandmum again," she whispered as she fell asleep.

During the night a strange thing occurred. Jessica found herself standing inside a long, dark hall with doors all along one side. She felt her grandmother standing near and she heard her whisper. "Don't be afraid. There's always a door to show you the way. All you need to have is the key. Come with me now and I'll show you the one that was waiting for me."

A door swung slowly open. Jessica blinked in the sudden light, then she stepped through.

Where am I now? It looks like our house. But everything seems different somehow. The trees are so small, the cars are strange and the pavement is gone from the street.

Oh! There's Grandmum! But she looks so young. How can that be? She's always been old and she can't walk that fast.

Grandmum, here! I'm over here!

She doesn't hear me calling. She doesn't see me either. It looks like she's going some place important. I'll follow a while and see.

She's getting on a funny-looking streetcar. I'd better get on too.

She still doesn't see me. Nobody does!

Why have we come to the railway station? Grandmum can't be taking a train. She hasn't even got a suitcase.

Look, there's Granddad. She's meeting him! He looks young too. But what's he wearing a uniform for? Why is Grandmum so sad?

I remember it now. He's going away to fight in the war. Grandmum's giving him her photograph. He hasn't got one to give to her. He's handing over the album instead.

Now it's time for his train to go. Grandmum's crying. I am too.

Don't worry Grandmum, he's going to come back!

We're home again now. Grandmum is smiling at Granddad's stamp. It does look a little bit like him.

Look what she's doing, look at that! She's opening up her silver locket. She's putting the stamp inside!

When Jessica woke the following day, she ran to the kitchen right away.

"I know where to find the stamp," she said, and she told her family where it was.

"Of course, that's it!" her granddad cried. "Grandmum put the missing stamp inside the locket instead of a photograph."

"Now don't get your hopes up," warned Jessica's mother. "You don't know for sure if the stamp's really there."

"It is," Jessica told her. "It's hard to explain, but I know."

Jessica used her grandfather's pocket knife to pry the clasp. It wasn't easy, but after a while the locket came open. Jessica could hardly believe her eyes when she saw what was inside.

"It's only a photograph!" she said.

"The one I gave her after the war," her granddad sighed.

Jessica put the locket down and tried not to show just how bad she felt. "I can't understand it," she told them all.

Jessica's mother gave her shoulder a squeeze. "Don't feel bad. You tried your best," she said gently.

Granddad picked up the locket and studied it for a while. Then he shook his head and sighed again. "Might as well take the photo out, Jess. Now that the locket is finally open, you'll want to put something of your own inside."

He grasped the picture and pulled it free. Something small and surprisingly familiar fell out from behind the photograph.

"That's it! That's the stamp!" Jessica cried.

"It certainly is," her granddad said with a grin a mile wide.

Jessica's dad and granddad went off to see how much money the stamp would bring. As it turned out, it was worth more than enough and a little bit extra besides.

Jessica tried for the rest of that day to decide what she wanted inside the locket. Nothing she had seemed right at all. Finally that night before going to sleep, she held the locket tight in her hand and closed her eyes. After a while her granddad came to say goodnight. He paused for a moment by the open door and gazed at Jessica's face. After a moment she opened her eyes.

"You look different tonight," he said to her. "For a moment there, you looked just like your grandmother."

Jessica looked up. "You look different too. More like you did before the war." Then she grinned. "We did it, Granddad. I knew we would. You weren't too old and I wasn't too young."

Her granddad smiled. "Do you know what goes in the locket yet?"

"No, I don't," she replied. "I was remembering what Grandmum said about doors and keys. What if a key isn't always a person? It was for Grandmum, but mine might be different. Grandmum would tell me to wait and see; that a key comes along when you're ready. I'm keeping the locket empty for now until what goes inside finds me."

"Your grandmother always gave good advice. It seems she still does," her granddad said. "I'm not too surprised. She was an amazing person, Jess, and so are you, you know."